The Lion and the Porcupine

The Story of an Amazing Friendship

by

Susan Liverpool

Illustrated by Cate Miller

First published by Friends of Faith

ISBN 978-1-939761-23-1
Printed in the United States of America

This book is printed on acid-free paper.

3255 Lawrenceville-Suwanee Rd.
Suite P250
Suwanee, GA 30024
publishing@faithbooksandmore.com
faithbooksandmore.com

Ordering Information:
Quantity sales. Special discounts are available on quantity purchases by corporations, associations, and others. For details, contact the publisher at the address above.

Orders by U.S. trade bookstores and wholesalers. Please contact Ingram Book Company: Tel: (800) 937-8000; Email: orders@ingrambook.com or visit ipage. ingrambook.com.
The Lion and the Porcupine Audiobook including 7 original songs composed by the author is available for purchase as a CD or as a download on **Amazon and iTunes.**

Disclaimer
The purpose of this book is to empower, educate, and offer hope. The authors of the book achieved that through their own experiences, expertise, and research. Consequently, this book should only be used as a road map. This book is not intended to be nor is it represented as legal advice. The authors are not liable or responsible, to any person, or entity, for any and all claims, demands, damages, causes of action, suits in equity of whatever kind or nature, caused or alleged to have been caused, directly or indirectly, by the information contained in this book or the authors' past or future negligence or wrongful acts.

For my son, Jason Hill, love always.
and
In loving memory of
Zion Malave,
who said, "He should have a real ruler!"

Love and Acknowledgments
(words can't express)

Joe Hampton
Ann Wilson
Zahava Kurland
Kathryn Copper
Rachael Siegelman
Verna Barksdale
Christine Malave
and
Susan Campus
who ignited the spark by saying... "You've got to write this story!"

Landmark Education, for providing the programs that rekindled my love of the Arts.

FOREWORD

How do a lion and a porcupine become friends? Very carefully!

In this charming story, the chance meeting of two unlikely acquaintances—a cranky lion and a brave but quirky porcupine—at first seems destined for disaster. But Susan Liverpool has invented a world where natural enemies find common ground in their loneliness and isolation. The songs she has written to accompany the story add an amazing dimension of liveliness and spice!

Susan believes "the arts are a ministry to the soul," and she practices what she preaches. When we nurture the artist in each of us, she says, we find opportunities—as both the lion and the porcupine did—to grow and embrace our differences.

-Ann Wilson
President
Maywood Marketing & Communications

Being King of the Jungle can sometimes be a lonely life. Who can I talk to? The Pride is always away hunting for food. And the other animals are beneath me. I can't be seen talking to a monkey or a giraffe. What would the other lions think?

So that's why (just between you and me), I let that strange little porcupine, with her sticky quills and musty smell, get near me in the first place!

I was feeling pretty moody that day, so I raised my paw to scare her away. But she kept inching closer to me. How DARE she come near the King of the Jungle, sniffing and muttering to herself! Was she crazy? Had she not been taught how to behave around royalty?

3

If I were seen giving the time of day to this odd little creature, why, my reputation would be ruined! Lions from all over the jungle would challenge me and try to steal my Pride!

So I

GROWLED

at her.

This seemed to startle the porcupine, but not enough to make her run and hide. Instead, she just sat there trembling, staring up at me with those big, watery eyes.

I stayed calm, but in my most threatening voice, I roared,

"WHY are YOU Here?"

"DON'T YOU KNOW WHO I AM?"

The little porcupine jumped, falling back on her prickly bottom. "Mr. King, I mean no harm. I lost my way. Please don't eat me!"

"You have also lost your mind, for I could end your life with just one swipe of my mighty paw! Don't you know that?" I snarled.

"I guess I should, but I was separated from my family when I was born and have been on my own ever since," she babbled. "I am still learning the ways of the jungle...

6

...Usually I avoid lions, but when I saw YOU, I thought to myself, this lion is different—
here is a wise and powerful king. He will help me find my family, and I'll never be lonely again!"

Can you believe this silliness? What irritating little creatures porcupines are! You can't get to their juicy
meat without getting all those quills stuck in your face (and your mouth), so it's useless to try to eat them!

I roared again,

"I am the KING of the Jungle"

"I don't HELP animals, I EAT animals! What makes you think I have time to bother with your petty problems?" Then I stood and walked away, swatting her with my tail. But her innocent pleas tugged at my heart. Here we were, two lonely creatures, different and yet the same...

"Wait a minute!" I thought. "I'm King of the Jungle! I can't LIKE a porcupine!"

8

9

Her squeaky little voice interrupted my thoughts. "Your Majesty, my name is

Penelope!!!

and if you'd be my friend, I could help you. Can I get a hug?"
I was flabbergasted! "No, you cannot have a hug, and what in the world do you think
YOU could do for ME? Why, if it weren't for your sticky little quills, I'd have eaten you by now!"

...tee hee hee!......

she giggled nervously, but I could tell the porcupine was thinking to herself,
"I'd like to see you try to take a bite out of me!" She fidgeted with her quills.

"Oh, Mr. King, you are

Hilarious!!!

You wouldn't really eat
a little porcupine, would you? I've heard that brave lions don't bother to eat creatures like me."
Now I was fed up with this little pest! The Pride would be home soon with the day's meal. If they saw me
hanging out with a porcupine, they'd leave, and there was nothing worse than a lion
who couldn't hold onto his "pride."

So I placed my giant paw under the porcupine and flipped her onto her back.
Mmmm... I could see her soft little belly. I watched as she wiggled and squirmed,
trying to turn herself back over. Then I drew close so she could see my blazing eyes
and feel the heat of my breath. My mouth was big enough to swallow her whole.
I let loose a growl from deep in my throat and roared,

"Now, I'll give you 2 seconds to tell me why I shouldn't bite your soft little belly and have you for an appetizer?!!

The little critter couldn't speak! Her teeth chattered
and her heart was pounding so loudly I could hear it.
"Y-y-your Majesty!" she finally sputtered. "I... I noticed
that your beautiful mane is all t-t-tangled.
You could use me as a comb.
My quills could straighten out your
lovely locks. I could even get rid of
all those little insects in your hair.

13

"Look—when my quills are flat like this, they won't stick you," she continued. "Mr. King, by the time I'm finished, your mane will be the envy of all the lions in the Kingdom! Lionesses will fight to be at your side!"

I was at a loss for words. Was she serious? I knew the little porcupine was begging for her life, but I just couldn't do away with her. I admired her courage, and she had appealed to my vanity. Alas, it was true. I couldn't remember the last time my mane had been properly combed. These days, the lionesses had no time to groom me like they used to. They were always busy on the hunt.

Why, just the other day, Lydia, my Number One wife, had said, "Times have changed, Lawrence." (Lydia is the only one allowed to call me by my real name.) "You can't expect us to hunt all day, and then come home and wait on you hand and foot. We'd like to be groomed, too, once in a while, you know!"

I carefully turned the little porcupine back onto her feet. She dusted herself off and tried to settle those quills, which were now completely out of control.

"All right!" I said. "Go ahead, groom me. But be warned! ...

...If you stick me just once, I will tear you apart! Do you understand, ummm... what was your name again?"

"...P...P...Penelope Your Majesty"

"Well, Penelope, get to it before the Pride returns, and I become the joke of the jungle!"

15

Penelope quickly climbed to the top of my head. "Wow! What a view from up here!" she said. "I can see for miles in every direction!" She gently lay on her back, slowly wiggling and rolling herself down my mane, carefully untangling my bushy hair. She worked hard, scurrying up and down, moving as fast as she could to finish the job.

16

"Oh, your Majesty!
You look

Magnificent!

Penelope smiled, as she admired her handiwork.

I realized I had no way of knowing whether I looked good or not. I'd have to trust the little creature. The reaction of the Pride would be the true test. If the lionesses laughed or backed away from me, well, I'd just have to make the porcupine disappear! I'd say the "thing" must have crawled upon me while I slept and got tangled up in my hair!

"Penelope, for your sake, I hope you're right. I've started to like you, and I'd hate to see anything happen to you... you know what I mean?"

The little porcupine gulped. "Y-y-yes, your Majesty," she whispered. "I, I know what you mean."

17

At that very moment, the lionesses returned from the hunt. Lydia was in the lead, carrying the day's meal in her powerful jaws. Penelope was still perched on top of my head. "Don't move," I whispered. She scrunched herself into a ball and lay very still.

Lydia slowly began circling me, her eyes wide with wonder. The other lionesses sat quietly at a distance, waiting for Lydia to signal that it was safe to come close.

"Lawrence— what happened to you?!"

"What do you mean, Lydia?" I replied calmly.

19

I knew Penelope wanted to poke out her head to see what was happening, but she didn't budge.
"Well, there's something different about you, Lawrence, and I can't quite put my paw on it," Lydia said.
I couldn't tell what she was thinking, so I roared, "Come on, Lydia, I'm King of the Jungle,
for goodness' sake!   Do you like my mane or not?"

Lydia knew it wouldn't be wise to growl at me in front of the other lionesses. I waited. I could feel Penelope squirming. She knew if Lydia hated my mane, she was doomed! As King, I would never say to Lydia or the lionesses that I had let a porcupine comb my hair!

21

Finally...

Lydia cleared her throat and said, "Lawrence—your mane! It's… it's… beautiful!
How did you get it to look like that?"

"It was nothing really," I sniffed. "I simply kidnapped this little porcupine"
(I waved my paw toward the top of my head) "and commanded her to groom me,
since YOU and the other lionesses seem to be too busy lately." Penelope popped her head
out and gave a respectful nod to Lydia.

Lydia was startled at first, then nodded back, smiled at me, and said, "Lawrence, groomed or not, you are as handsome to me now as you were the day we met."
Then she nuzzled her head against my shoulder.

Penelope jumped for joy! I gently lowered my head and said,
"Penelope, stop dancing on my head and come down here please. I want to talk with you."

24

25

Hearing the kindness in my voice, Penelope
slid down my mane, letting out a big Whee!!!...

...as she tumbled to the ground and landed in front of my nose.
I looked at her, rolled my eyes and muttered,
"Heaven help this poor little creature...
and me.

"Penelope, I know you want to find YOUR family, but what if you joined OUR family?" I said softly.

Her large brown eyes began to fill with tears.

"Oh for goodness' sake, Penelope, you're not going to cry, are you?"

"No, Sire," she whispered. "It's just that I've never really had a family before. Are you sure you want me?"

Yes Penelope... we want You!!!

28

"Yes, Penelope," Lydia spoke up. "We want you. Come travel with us. Who knows? Maybe we'll meet up with your family, and if we don't, you're welcome to stay with us.

"You could groom all of us, not just the King. We lionesses like to look good, too, you know! Why, you wouldn't believe how messy our hair gets when we're out hunting!"

"Yeah," another lioness chimed in, "not to mention what hunting day after day does to our claws." The other lionesses nodded and smiled.

"Well... what do you say Penelope?!!"

I said, as I strolled toward the Pride. "We can have exciting talks while the lionesses are on the hunt, and you can sit on top of my head as much as you want... as long as there aren't any other lions around, of course."

Penelope scurried along beside me, listening and giggling.
By now her quills were all over the place, but I could tell she didn't care.

Life had taken a strange and wonderful turn for Penelope and me.

She hadn't found the family she was looking for.
She had found a family that was beyond her wildest dreams!

As for me, I had done something I never imagined I could do. I had made a friend.

THE END

About the Author

The Lion and the Porcupine is Susan Liverpool's second book and her first for children. Born and raised in Chicago, Susan grew up singing and has always been passionate about the Arts. More recently, she has discovered her gift for songwriting, composing a series of can't-get-them-out-of-your-head tunes to accompany both her first book, The Little Liverpool Diaries, and The Lion and the Porcupine. She also has published three books of poetry.

Photo by Asa Murray

Susan holds a bachelor's degree in nursing from the University of Illinois. She has a son, Jason Hill, and lives in Atlanta, Georgia.

About the Illustrator

Cate Miller grew up in an artistic family and has always had a passion for the visual arts. She began her career in print advertising and later became an art teacher. There was no going back.

This is Cate's first picture book and a new adventure! She loves the energy and creativity of young people, and after years of enjoying beautiful picture book illustrations and stories, she feels fortunate to have met Susan Liverpool and been introduced to her charming story and songs. The journey to bring Penelope and Lawrence to life has been fun to share with her supportive family and friends, especially her three creative daughters.

CPSIA information can be obtained at www.ICGtesting.com
Printed in the USA
LVIW01n1444140115
422793LV00004B/7